Birthday Wishes for BRODY

by Suzanne Marshall

LiveWellMedia.com

ISBN-13: 978-1544056401
ISBN-10: 1544056400

This book is dedicated to

who is loved very much!

Brody,

the bees are buzzing
with the news
of birthday wishes
just for you.

Brody,
a panda plays a birthday song,
wishing you joy the whole day long!

Brody,
a fish has this birthday
wish for you:
"May all your happy
dreams come true."

Brody,

a lively pony trotting your way
wishes you strength to stand and say
"I can do it!" every day.

Brody,

a piggy wishes you lots of pluck.
So when you fall, you rise back up.

Brody,

an elephant has this wish for you:
a bright and positive attitude
to fill your heart with gratitude.

HAPPY BIRTHDAY

Brody,
a groundhog pops up to say:
"More birthday wishes
are on the way!"

Brody,

a lion wishes you lots of smiles,
since smiles never go out of style.

Happy Birthday

Brody,

playful monkeys wearing hats
wish you giggles, chuckles and laughs.

Brody,
birthday wishes
from a tiger cub
include plenty of kisses
and plenty of hugs.

Happy Birthday

Brody,
a lamb makes a wish
that has already come true:
lots and lots of love for you!

Happy
Birthday

A dog and cat exclaim with glee:
"Brody is loved to the utmost degree.
Brody is loved to infinity!"

Brody,

all your friends come out to say:
"Hip, hip, hooray, and happy birthday!
We love you, Brody, every day."

Your birthday love never ends.
So pass it on to family and friends.
Spread birthday love to ALL with cheer.
Spread birthday love throughout the year!

Happy birthday Brody!

Special Thanks

to my parents for their love and support, and to my awesome editorial team: Hannah & Rachel Roeder, and Don Marshall. Artwork has been edited by the author. Original scenes: © Colematt, © Tigatelu, © Bluering (fotosearch.com). Original cat, chicks, dog, fish, groundhog, lamb, lion, panda, pony, tiger: © Dazdraperma (fotosearch.com). Original bee, elephant, monkeys & pig: © Tigatelu (fotosearch.com). Additional images curated from freepik.com.

About the Author

An honors graduate of Smith College, Suzanne Marshall writes to engage and empower children. Her children's books are full of positive affirmations and inspirational quotes. Learn more about Suzanne and her books at: LiveWellMedia.com.

Made in the USA
Monee, IL
29 September 2023